For my own dear, superfast HumFree; you
continue to teach me everything I know about
being the best mama I can be as well as a voice
for those who need us. I love you and the light
you bring to my life — A.J.

Acknowledgements

Special thanks to my husband for believing in me;
to Brian Talbott for bringing HumFree to life so
beautifully; to the Mascot Books team for their support,
to Kristin Beltaos for her insight and to Alix Reeves for
her unfailing encouragement.

Foreword

HumFree was inspired by my son, whose joyful
enthusiasm for playing, running and being "super fast"
while bravely handling the day-to-day ups and downs
of food allergies makes me so proud. I hope HumFree's
story will serve as a helpful foundation of food allergy
awareness and education, starting with our most
important members: our precious children. A portion of
my proceeds will be dedicated to supporting our food
allergy community.

Library of Congress Control Number: 2015909569

CPSIA Code: PRT0815A
ISBN-13: 9781620865446

Printed in the United States

www.mascotbooks.com

HumFree the Bee

Has a Food Allergy

Alison Grace Johansen

Illustrations by
Brian Talbott

There once was a baby bee
Named HumFree, as cute as could be.

He could fly as high as the tallest tree
And buzz louder than a symphony.

The only thing HumFree just couldn't do
Was land on flowers that were yellow or blue.
No matter how hard he tried,
He'd sneeze!

AHHH-CHOOOOOOO!

He tried being slow.

He tried being fast.

He tried landing first.

He tried landing last.

But oh, no matter what HumFree would do,
He just couldn't be near
those yellows and blues.

He'd gasp! He'd cough!

He'd sneeze!

AHHH-CHOOOOOOOO!

He cried, "Mama, oh Mama, what should I do?

My wings are itchy and my belly hurts, too!

Mama, oh Mama, how can this be?

How will my friends fly with me?"

Sweet little HumFree,
the baby bee
Couldn't touch or eat
the pollen, you see.

With just one bite, he was as sick as could be.
HumFree the bee had a food allergy.

"HumFree, don't worry!
There are things you can do."
His mama said, "Your cousin
has a food allergy, too.

Instead of landing on yellow or blue, she lands on pink and green!

Everyone is amazed. She's the fastest bee they've ever seen!"

"What?" HumFree cried. "That's great! Yippee!
Now all my friends can fly with me!"

He landed on orange, purple and green!
He was amazing–the fastest they'd seen!

Now he could be slow.

Now he could be fast.

Now he could land first.

Now he could land last.

He learned to say, "BUZZ OFF!
Those blues aren't for me!

NO THANK YOU!
'Cause I have a food allergy."

And hey! He could breathe!
And his throat wasn't itchy!

And he didn't sneeze!
And his wings weren't all twitchy!

"Woo-hoo!" HumFree cried.

"Look at me!
BUZZ-AREEEEEE!

I feel so much better!
I can fly, fast and free!"

His friends helped to keep him as safe as could be.
He felt loved and included! Imagine his glee!

HumFree was as happy as a bee could be
Once he learned how to fly safely with a food allergy.

HumFree's Food Allergy Bee: Think "A-E-I-O-U"

A is for Awareness!

Keep your friends safe! Spread the word!
Tell your friends and family everything you've learned!

Q: Do you have a friend or family member with a food allergy? Do you have a food allergy?

A: About 15 million Americans, including 5.9 million children, have food allergies and this number is on the rise. This means about 1 in every 13 kids or about 2 children in every classroom.* Know that if you have a food allergy, YOU ARE NOT ALONE!

E is for Education!

Arm yourselves with knowledge! "Bee" your very best!

Q: HumFree is allergic to the pollen, or protein, in blue and yellow flowers. What are your friends' food allergies? What are yours?

A: COW'S MILK, EGG, SOY, WHEAT, PEANUT, TREE NUT, SHELLFISH and FISH are the top 8 most common food allergens, but any food, drink or product (such as soap, lotion or even art supplies like paint) may be or contain allergens.

Q: What should we do if someone is having an allergic reaction?

A: Our friends with food allergies should always have two epinephrine auto-injectors with them. This can be life-saving medicine. If someone is having an allergic reaction, quickly find an adult to help and call 9-1-1. EVERY SECOND COUNTS!

I is for INCLUSION:

"Bee" nice! Let's make it safe,
so everyone can celebrate!

Q: How can we make play dates, snack time and other gatherings safe?

A: Just as HumFree can't touch or eat the pollen in blue and yellow flowers, our friends with food allergies can't eat or touch their allergens. HumFree and his friends keep blue and yellow pollen from touching his flowers, or cross-pollinating. If food or drinks are at a gathering, keep them and other items like utensils and cups safe from cross-contamination. Don't share or trade food! Wash your hands after eating! Hand sanitizers do not remove food allergen proteins.

O is for OUTREACH!
U is for UNDERSTANDING!

Let's help our friends! Let's all reach out!
Let's show we know what it's all about!

Q: How can we reach out so everyone feels included?

A: Ask your friends what's safe for them!
Show them you understand and care. There are tons of super cool crafts, games, activities and prizes that are food-free and fun to share! HumFree says to "bee" a good friend! "Bee" creative!

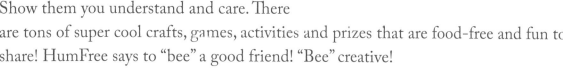

Food Allergy Research & Education provides these statistics and more at: foodallergy.org.

Alison Johansen is a freelance writer who spent several years working as a legal reporter and editor in Washington, D.C. She lives in Northern Virginia with her husband and two children. When her son was diagnosed with multiple food allergies, her family began their journey of managing an ever changing and challenging area of pediatric health. Find out more about Alison by visiting her website, Mothernova.com; following her on Twitter @Mothernova; and liking her at Facebook.com/Mothernova.